STORIES FROM THE FIVE TOWNS

Bursley, Hanbridge, Knype, Longshaw, Turnhill – these are the Five Towns of Arnold Bennett's stories, set in the English Midlands in the early 1900s. Today the Five Towns are the city of Stoke-on-Trent, but the place is still famous for its pottery . . . and for the people in Arnold Bennett's stories.

They are not famous or important people. They work in shops and factories; they fall in, and out of, love; they argue and they quarrel. Sometimes they are clever and successful, and sometimes they do very stupid things. Philip has some important news to tell his mother, but he is also going to get a big surprise . . . Sir Jee hates his portrait, but what can he do about it? It was a present from the people of the Five Towns . . . At Knype station, Toby Hall suddenly decides to take the train to Turnhill, but why? Then there are John and Robert. They are brothers, they live in the same house, they eat meals together – and neither has said a single word to the other for ten years . . .

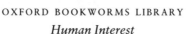

OXFORD BOOKWORMS LIBRARY
Human Interest

Stories from the Five Towns

Stage 2 (700 headwords)

Series Editor: Jennifer Bassett
Founder Editor: Tricia Hedge
Activities Editors: Jennifer Bassett and Alison Baxter

ARNOLD BENNETT

Stories from the Five Towns

Retold by
Nick Bullard

OXFORD UNIVERSITY PRESS
2000

Oxford University Press,
Great Clarendon Street, Oxford OX2 6DP

Oxford New York
Athens Auckland Bangkok Bogotá Buenos Aires Calcutta Cape Town
Chennai Dar es Salaam Delhi Florence Hong Kong Istanbul Karachi
Kuala Lumpur Madrid Melbourne Mexico City Mumbai Nairobi
Paris São Paulo Singapore Taipei Tokyo Toronto Warsaw
and associated companies in
Berlin Ibadan

OXFORD and OXFORD ENGLISH
are trade marks of Oxford University Press

ISBN 0 19 422986 6

Illustrated by Martin Hargreaves

Printed in Spain by Unigraf s.l.

CONTENTS

My mother never came to meet me at Bursley station when I arrived in the Five Towns from London. She always had other things to do; she was getting ready for me. So I always walked alone up Trafalgar Road, between the factories and past the football field. And so tonight, I had time to

I always walked alone up Trafalgar Road.

1

think. I had some very important news for my mother, and I didn't know how to tell her.

I wrote to my mother every week, to tell her what I was doing. She knew the names of all my friends. I often wrote about Agnes and her family. But it's difficult to write in a letter: 'I think Agnes likes me,' 'I'm in love with her,' 'I'm sure she likes me,' 'I think she loves me,' 'I'm going to ask her to marry me.' You can't do that. Well, I couldn't do it. And on the 20th December I asked Agnes to marry me, and Agnes said yes. But my mother didn't know anything about it. And now, on the 22nd December, I was coming to spend Christmas with my mother.

My mother was a widow. I was her only son – and now I was engaged and she didn't know. I was afraid she was going to be a little unhappy, and I was ready for a difficult evening.

I walked up to the front door, but before I put my hand up to ring, the door opened and there was my mother. She put her arms around me.

'Well, Philip! How are you?'

And I said, 'Oh! I'm all right, mother. How are you?'

She smiled at me. She looked excited and younger than her forty-five years. There was something strange in her smile. I thought: 'She *knows* I'm going to get married. How does she know?'

But I said nothing. You have to be careful with mothers.

2

'I'll tell her at supper,' I decided.

I went upstairs to my bedroom. When I came down, my mother was busy in the kitchen. I went into the dining-room, and here I had a surprise. There were three chairs around the table, and three plates and three glasses.

So Agnes *was* coming! I didn't know how my mother knew, but she did know. She and my wonderful Agnes were planning a surprise for me. Agnes was coming to Bursley for Christmas!

There was a ring at the door. 'It's Agnes!' I thought, and running to the door, I opened it.

It was Mr Nixon.

Mr Nixon was an old friend of the family. He was a large, strong man of about forty-nine or fifty. He was very helpful to my mother after my father's death.

'Good evening, young man,' he said. 'It's good to see you back in Bursley.'

'Mr Nixon has come for supper, Philip,' said my mother.

Mr Nixon often came to supper during my visits to Bursley, but never on the first night. I liked him, but I wasn't very happy to see him tonight because I wanted to talk to my mother. I couldn't talk to her about Agnes with Mr Nixon sitting at the table.

We started our supper. We talked about this and that, but nobody ate very much. I was thinking about what to say to my mother when Mr Nixon went home. At the end of the meal I told my mother that I must go to the post office. I had an important letter to post.

'Can't it wait until tomorrow, my pet?' my mother asked.

'It can't,' I said.

My letter, of course, was to Agnes. A letter to Agnes could not wait until tomorrow! I walked over to the dining-room door.

'A letter to a lady?' asked Mr Nixon, laughing.

'Yes,' I replied.

I walked to the post office and posted my letter. When I got back home, I was sorry to see that Mr Nixon was still there. He was alone in the sitting-room, smoking.

'Where's mother?' I asked.

'She's just gone out of the room,' he said. 'Come and sit down. Have a cigarette. I'd like to talk to you, Philip.'

I took a cigarette and sat down. I hoped the talk was not going to be a long one.

'Well, my boy,' he said. 'Would you like me as a stepfather?'

For a second I could not move or speak.

'What?' I said. 'You mean . . . you and my mother . . .?'

'Yes, my boy, I do. I asked her yesterday, and she said yes. I've wanted to ask her for a long time – I think she knew that. Did she tell you in her letters? No? It's difficult to write in a letter, of course. She couldn't really write,

"My dear Philip, an old friend, Mr Nixon, is falling in love with me and I think I'm falling in love with him. I think he'll ask me to marry him soon." I don't think your mother could write that, could she?'

I laughed.

'Shake hands,' I said. 'This is wonderful news.'

After a moment my mother came in, a little red in the face.

'The boy's very happy, Sarah,' said Mr Nixon.

After a moment my mother came in.

I said nothing about my own plans that evening. It was something new to me that my mother could fall in love, and that a man could fall in love with her. It was something new to me that she was lonely in our old house and that perhaps she wanted a new life. Perhaps, like all sons, I thought only about myself and my life. So I decided to say nothing about my news, and that evening my mother came first for me. I could tell her about Agnes tomorrow. We live and learn.

THE BURGLARY

Lady Dain said: 'Jee, if that portrait stays there much longer, I shall go mad. I can't eat any more with it up there!' She looked up at the big portrait on the wall opposite the breakfast table.

Sir Jehoshaphat said nothing.

Lady Dain did not like the portrait. Nobody in the Five Towns liked the portrait. But the portrait was by Cressage, the finest portrait painter in England, and a portrait by Cressage cost a thousand pounds or more.

'I can't eat any more with it up there!'

Sir Jehoshaphat Dain was perhaps the cleverest and most successful businessman in the Five Towns. His business, called Dain Brothers, had one of the biggest pottery factories in England, and their cups and plates went all over the world. Sir Jehoshaphat was rich, because he sold his pottery very cheaply, and paid his workers very little. But Sir Jee liked to be important, so he used some of his money to pay for schools and hospitals for the people of the Five Towns.

The people of the Five Towns often laughed at Sir Jee, but they also wanted to say thank you for the schools and hospitals. They decided to give him a portrait for a present. So Cressage painted the portrait and many people in London thought it was very good. 'A wonderfully clever portrait of a successful businessman from a small town; a little man who has made a lot of money and who thinks he is very important,' said one newspaper.

It was not a kind portrait and many of the people of the Five Towns laughed when they saw it. But Sir Jehoshaphat had to take his present, and to say thank you for it. Now it was on his wall in his home, Sneyd Castle, and after sixteen months Lady Dain was tired of looking at it.

'Don't be stupid, wife,' said Sir Jee. 'I'm not taking that portrait down, or selling it – not even for ten thousand pounds. I want to keep it.'

But that wasn't true. Sir Jee hated the portrait more than

his wife did. And he was thinking of a secret plan to get rid of it.

'Are you going into town this morning?' asked his wife.

'Yes,' he answered. 'I'm in court today.'

He was one of the town magistrates. While he travelled into town, he thought about his plan for the portrait. It was a wild and dangerous plan, but he thought it was just possible.

■ ■ ■ ■ ■

That morning, the police were very angry with Sir Jee. A man was in court, and the police said he was a burglar. They wanted him to go to prison for five years or more. But Sir Jee did not agree. He said there was no proof that William Smith was a burglar. The other magistrate was very surprised at this and the police were very cross, but William Smith left the court a free man. Before he left, Sir Jee asked to see him in his office.

'Smith,' said Sir Jee, looking at him carefully, 'you were a lucky man this morning, you know.'

Smith was a small, thin man, with untidy hair and dirty clothes.

'Yes, I was lucky,' he answered. 'And what do you want from me?'

'I hope I can help you,' said Sir Jee.

'I don't know if I want help, but I never say no to money.'

'Sit down,' said Sir Jee.

William Smith sat down at Sir Jee's desk. 'Well?' he asked.

'I want you to steal something from my house. But it won't be a crime.'

'What?' Smith was very surprised.

'In my house, Sneyd Castle, there is a portrait of myself. I want someone to steal it.'

'Steal it?'

'Yes.'

'I want you to steal something from my house.'

'How much will you pay me for doing it?'

'Pay you?' said Sir Jee. 'It's a Cressage! You'll get two thousand pounds for it in America.'

And Sir Jee told Smith the story of the portrait and why he wanted to get rid of it. Smith thought for a minute and then said:

'All right, I'll do it, just to help you.'

'When can you do it? Tonight?'

'No,' said Smith. 'I'm busy tonight.'

'Well, tomorrow night.'

'I'm busy tomorrow, too.'

'You're a busy man,' said Sir Jee.

'Well, business is business, you know,' said Smith. 'I can do it the day after tomorrow.'

'But that's Christmas Eve.'

'Well, it's either that or Christmas Day. I'm busy again after that.'

'Not in the Five Towns, I hope,' said Sir Jee.

'No. There's nothing left in the Five Towns.'

So they agreed on Christmas Eve.

'Now,' said Sir Jee, 'I'll describe the rooms in Sneyd Castle to you. Then you'll know where—'

William Smith looked at him and laughed loudly. 'Describe the rooms to me? Do you think I'm stupid? I'm a businessman – I know Sneyd Castle better than you do.'

■ ■ ■ ■ ■

On the afternoon of 24th December, when Sir Jehoshaphat came home to Sneyd Castle, his wife was packing suitcases. The Dains were going to their son's house for Christmas. Their son John had a new wife and a new baby, and he wanted to spend Christmas in his new home with all the family.

'Oh, Jee!' she cried. 'You are difficult.'

Sir Jee said nothing to his wife immediately. He watched her for a while and then later, during tea, he said suddenly:

'I can't come to John's house this afternoon.'

'Oh, Jee!' she cried. 'You *are* difficult. Why didn't you tell me before?'

He didn't answer the question. 'I'll come over tomorrow morning – perhaps in time for church.'

'There's no food in the house. And the servants are all going away on holiday. There's nobody to cook for you. I'll stay with you if you like.'

'No, I'll be all right.'

Lady Dain went to her son's, leaving some cold food for Sir Jee.

Sir Jee had a cold, silent meal, in front of his portrait. He was alone in the castle and that was a good thing, he decided. There were no servants to wake up and hear William Smith at work. Sir Jee was a little afraid; perhaps it was dangerous to bring a burglar into the house. He looked again at the portrait in its big gold frame. 'Will he take the frame?' he asked himself. 'I hope he doesn't. It's very heavy. I don't think one man could carry that.' But perhaps Smith had someone to help him.

'Goodbye!' he said to his portrait, opened one of the windows for William Smith, and went to bed.

He did not sleep. He listened. At about two o'clock there were a few noises. They stopped, then started again. Smith

*Two men were carrying something large and square
across the garden.*

was at work. Sir Jee got out of bed quietly, went to the
window and looked out carefully. Two men were carrying
something large and square across the garden. So Smith
had a friend, and he was taking the portrait *and* the frame.

Sir Jee went back to bed. He slept for a few hours and
then went downstairs.

The portrait was on the floor with some writing across
it in big white letters: 'This is no good to me.' It was the
big gold frame that was missing.

And that wasn't all. Plates, knives, forks, spoons, cups
– everything made of silver was also missing. There was
not a single silver spoon left in the castle.

We are slow, silent people, we of the Five Towns. Perhaps it is because we make pottery, which is slow, silent work. There are many stories about us and how slow and silent we are. These stories often surprise the rest of the world very much, but we just laugh at them. Here is an example.

Toby Hall was born in Turnhill, the smallest of the Five Towns. Last New Year's Eve he was travelling by train from Crewe to Derby, which was now his home town. He got out of the train at Knype, in the centre of the Five Towns, for a quick drink. The station was busy and he had to wait for his drink. When he returned to the train, it

The station was busy and he had to wait for his drink.

was already moving. Toby was not a young man; he couldn't jump on the train, so he missed it.

He went to speak to the man in the station office. 'Young man,' he asked. 'When's the next train to Derby?'

'There isn't one before tomorrow.'

Toby went and had another drink.

'I'll go to Turnhill,' he said to himself slowly, and he paid for his drink.

This was his first visit to the Five Towns for twenty-three years, but Knype station was still the same, and so were the times of the trains to Turnhill. The train was the same, too.

In twenty minutes he was leaving Turnhill station and walking into the town. He walked past a number of fine new buildings. In the town centre almost everything was different.

He walked on, into smaller streets, and at last came to Child Row. The old houses here were the same as always, and he looked at one small house very carefully. The light was on, so there was somebody at home.

He crossed the street to the house. It was a special house for him (Number 11 it was – and is) because twenty-four years ago it was his home.

■ ■ ■ ■ ■

Twenty-four years ago, Toby Hall married Miss Priscilla Bratt, a quiet woman of twenty-three. The house belonged

The light was on, so there was somebody at home.

to her. The two young people were perhaps not really in love, but they liked one another. Their only problem was the house. Priscilla often said that the house belonged to her. Toby knew that. Everybody in Turnhill knew that. She didn't have to say it so often. Toby asked her not to, but she didn't stop. He was happy to live in his wife's house, but he didn't want to hear about it every day. And after a year it was too much. One day he put some things in a bag, put on his hat, and went to the door.

'Where are you going?' asked Priscilla.

He stopped for a minute, then answered, 'America.'

And he went. It was not difficult for Priscilla. She did not think that Toby was a very good husband. She could live without him; she had her house and some money.

Toby went to the bank and got all his money, and sailed off to New York on the *Adriatic*. From New York he went to Trenton, New Jersey, which was the Five Towns of America. Toby was a good potter, and he found work easily. After a year, he asked a friend to write to Priscilla, and tell her that he was dead. He wanted to be a free man, and it was only fair for her to be a free woman.

After a few years he returned to England. He changed his name from Hall, and started work as a potter in Derby. He did well – the money was good, and he didn't have much to spend it on. He lived quietly, working all week and going fishing at the weekends.

And now, because of a visit to Crewe, a train, and a drink, he was in Child Row, and crossing the street to Number 11. He knocked on the door.

■ ■ ■ ■ ■

Many doors in the Five Towns open slowly and carefully – and so did this one. It opened a few centimetres, and a woman looked out at Toby.

'Is this Mrs Hall's?' he asked.

'No. It's not Mrs Hall's. It's Mrs Tansley's.'

'I thought . . .'

The door opened a little more.

'Is that you, Toby?'

'It is,' answered Toby, smiling a little.

'Well, well!' said the woman. 'Well, well!' The door opened a little more. 'Are you coming in, Toby?'

'Yes,' said Toby.

And he went in.

'Sit down,' said his wife. 'I thought you were dead. Someone wrote to me.'

'Yes!' said Toby. 'But I'm not dead.'

He sat down in a comfortable chair by the fire. He knew the chair, and he knew the fire. He put his hat on the table. Priscilla locked the door again and sat down herself. Her dress was black and, like Toby, she was getting a little fat.

'Well, well,' she said. 'So you've come back.'

'Yes.'

19

'The weather's cold, isn't it?'

They were both silent for a minute.
'The weather's cold, isn't it?' he said.
'Yes. It's been a cold winter.'

Another silence. What were they thinking and feeling? Perhaps they weren't thinking anything very much.

'And what's the news?' he asked.

'News? Oh, nothing special.'

There was a picture above the fire. It was a picture of Priscilla when she was young. It surprised Toby.

'I don't remember that picture,' he said.

'What?'

'That!' He looked up at the picture.

'Oh! *That!* That's my daughter.'

'Oh!' Now Toby was surprised.

'I married Job Tansley,' said Priscilla. 'He died four years ago. She's married,' she said, looking up at her daughter's photograph. 'She married young Gibson last September.'

'Well, well!'

They were silent again.

'That's a good fire,' said Toby, looking at it.

'Yes, it is.'

'Good coal.'

'Seventy pence a tonne.'

Again they were silent.

'Is Ned Walklate still at the pub?' Toby asked.

'I think so,' said Priscilla.

'I think I'll go round and have a drink,' said Toby, standing up.

He was unlocking the door when Priscilla said:

'You've forgotten your hat, Toby.'

'You've forgotten your hat, Toby.'

'No,' he answered. 'I haven't forgotten it. I'm coming back.'

They looked at one another, speaking without words.

'That'll be all right,' she said. 'Well, well!'

'Yes!'

And he walked round to the pub.

John and Robert Hessian, brothers and bachelors, sat together after supper in their house in Oldcastle Street, Bursley. Both brothers were wearing black, because of the death of their older sister three months ago.

Maggie, the servant, came in to take the supper things off the table.

'Leave the coffee, Maggie,' said John, the elder brother, 'Mr Liversage is coming to visit.'

'Yes, Mr John,' said Maggie.

'Slate, Maggie,' said Robert.

'Yes, Mr Robert,' said Maggie.

The slate was on a table near the fire. Maggie gave it, and its pencil, to Robert.

Maggie gave it, and its pencil, to Robert.

Robert wrote: *Why is Liversage coming?*

And he pushed the slate across the table to John.

John wrote on the slate: *I don't know. He telephoned. He said he wanted to see us tonight.*

And he pushed the slate back to Robert.

John was forty-two years old, and Robert thirty-nine. They were tall, dark men, and both were well and strong. And there was nothing wrong with their hearing.

Ten years before, the brothers had a quarrel. The quarrel was a stupid one, like many quarrels. The morning after, Robert did not answer when John said something to him. 'Well,' said John to himself. 'If he doesn't speak, I won't speak.' And then Robert thought the same thing.

Maggie was the first to see that the brothers were not speaking. Then it was their best friend, Mr Liversage, the solicitor, and some of their other friends. But nobody said anything to them. The people of Bursley thought it was funny, and wanted to know which brother would win the quarrel. So Bursley watched the two men carefully, waiting for one of them to speak. But for ten years the brothers went on living together in the same house, and neither man spoke a single word to the other.

Life without words was very difficult for the brothers, but it was also difficult for their servant. Maggie gave them the slate, because it was easier for her when the brothers wrote things down. It was difficult for their friends too.

*Every evening Bursley watched the two brothers
while they walked home.*

They began to be a little bored when, at parties, each Hessian talked to everybody in the room – but not to his brother.

There was just one thing wrong with this beautiful quarrel. The brothers worked together in the same pottery factory, and sometimes they needed to speak on business. But they spoke very coldly, and only inside the factory walls. And every evening Bursley watched the two brothers while they walked home, one man five metres behind the other. How stupid it was! But Bursley said nothing.

The conversation by slate that evening was just finishing, when there was a knock at the door, and Mr Powell Liversage came in. He was an old friend of the two from their schooldays. He was also a bachelor, so his evenings were free. He came to see the Hessians every Saturday night, and usually John or Robert went to see him on Wednesdays. But today was Thursday.

'How are you?' asked John, lighting a cigarette.

'Well,' replied Liversage.

'How are you, Powell?' asked Robert.

'Not too bad. And you?'

He sat down and Robert gave him a cup of coffee.

'Well,' said Liversage, after a minute. He sounded a little uncomfortable. 'We've found your sister's will at last.'

'You haven't! When?' asked John.

'This afternoon. It was with some old papers in the bank.

Did you know that she had more than twelve thousand pounds?'

'No!' said Robert.

The brothers knew that their sister, Mrs Mary Bott, was rich. They knew that she had no children, and they knew, of course, that they were her only brothers. When she died three months ago, nobody could find her will. And now here it was! Twelve thousand pounds between two people was a lot of money for each of them. But what did the will say?

The two men wanted to know very much, but did they ask the question? Oh no! Neither man wanted to be the first to speak. And so they sat in silence.

'Do you want me to read the will to you?' asked Liversage at last.

'Yes,' they both answered.

Liversage took the will out of his pocket. 'Now, I didn't make this will,' he said, 'so please don't get angry with me.' This is what he read.

You are both very stupid, John and Robert, and I've often said so. Nobody understands why you quarrelled like that about Annie Emery. *Your* life is difficult, but you've also been very unkind to Annie. She's waited ten years already. So, John, if you marry Annie Emery, I shall give all my money to you. And Robert, if you marry her, I shall give it all to you. And you must be married in twelve months' time. And if neither of you marry her, then I give all my money to Miss Annie Emery, businesswoman, of Duck Bank, Bursley.

Mary Ann Bott, widow

'There. That's all.'

28

'There. That's all,' Liversage finished.

'Let me see,' said John. Liversage gave him the will and he looked at it carefully.

Robert walked around the table and looked at the paper in his brother's hand.

All three men were silent for a few minutes. Each was afraid to speak, and even afraid to look at the others.

'Well, I must go,' said Liversage, standing up.

'I say,' said Robert. 'You won't say anything about this to Annie, will you?'

'I will say nothing,' agreed Liversage. (But it was wrong of him to say this, because Annie already knew.)

The two brothers sat and thought for a long time.

Ten years before, when Annie was a woman of twenty-three, without family, she started a business for herself, which was a bookshop. John was in love with her, but so was Robert. And the two men quarrelled. They said very unkind, very unbrotherly things, and they were both very angry. Because of this (and because they were stupid), they each decided *not* to marry Annie. Each man wanted to show the other that *he* was the better, kinder, nicer brother. And so they did not speak for ten years. And poor Annie Emery, who wanted to marry one of the two (but could not decide which) did not marry anyone.

At two o'clock in the morning, John took a penny out of his pocket.

'Who shall go first?'

'Who shall go first?' he asked.

Robert felt very strange. His elder brother was speaking to him for the first time for ten years. For a minute he couldn't speak. John tossed the penny and put his hand over it.

'Heads or tails?' he asked.

'Tails,' said Robert.

But it was heads.

■ ■ ■ ■ ■

On Friday evening John knocked on the side door of Annie Emery's shop. While he stood there, he began to feel afraid. He still wanted to marry Annie, that was true. But how could he explain the last ten years? He began to hope that Annie was not there.

But the door opened, and there she was.

'Mr Hessian!' she cried, with a bright smile.

'I was just walking down Duck Bank,' he said. 'And I thought . . .'

And in fifteen seconds he was inside the house, sitting down.

'Mr Hessian!' she cried.

31

'But you're in the middle of eating your supper,' he said. He could see the food ready on the table.

'I haven't started,' she replied. 'Have you had your supper?'

'No,' he said.

'It will be nice of you to help me eat my supper, then,' said she.

'Oh! No . . .'

But she got plates and glasses out of the cupboard – and there he was, sitting at her table! He could not say no. It was wonderful.

'I'm doing well,' he thought. 'Poor Robert!'

He watched her while she moved about the room. He still did not know how to explain the ten silent years, but perhaps he didn't have to say anything. She was friendly, smiling, and pleased to see him, wasn't she? And she was still a beautiful woman – and also a good businesswoman.

He stayed, and they talked. He decided to ask her to marry him in a few days. Fifteen minutes later he thought about asking her the next day. And in another five minutes he was asking her to marry him, then and there.

She moved away from him quickly.

'It's very sudden. I must think about it,' she answered.

How happy he was! Her answer would soon be yes, he was sure.

'Will you be at church on Sunday?' she asked.

'Yes.'

'If my answer is yes, I shall wear white flowers in my hat. I prefer to give you my answer like that, without words. And if I am not at church next week, I will be the week after.'

'I understand,' he said. 'And if I do see those flowers, perhaps I can come to tea?'

'Yes. But you mustn't speak to me when I come out of church.'

He walked home down Oldcastle Street. He was a happy man – and he felt much younger than his forty-two years.

■ ■ ■ ■ ■

She was not at church on Sunday. Robert was away on business most of the week, and John was alone in the house. For many hours he sat at home, thinking about the next Sunday. Robert returned home on Friday.

On Sunday morning, John was up early. He put on his new shirt, which came from the best shop in Hanbridge. Robert was also out of bed early, and he was wearing a new shirt and a new suit. They had a silent breakfast.

'I'm going to church this morning, Maggie,' said Robert, finishing his breakfast. 'Where are my new shoes?'

This was a surprise. Robert did not usually go to church.

They walked to church, with John fifty metres in front of his brother. When he came into the church, Miss Emery was not there. The service was beginning when she walked

Her hat was like a garden.

in. She was wearing white flowers on her hat! There were about a hundred and fifty-five white flowers – her hat was like a garden.

How excited John was! He had Annie, and he had his sister's money. He felt very happy, and he decided to give five thousand pounds to Robert. Perhaps even a little more.

After the service John did not speak to Annie, but hurried home. Robert also went home, and then the two had their lunch. They didn't speak, of course; they read their newspapers.

After lunch they went out for a walk; not together, of course. John walked because he had to do something until his tea with Annie at half past four. And at half past four he turned the corner into Duck Bank – and saw Robert, who was coming round the corner at the other end of Duck Bank. They met outside Annie's door.

'What are you doing here?' asked Robert angrily.

'I'm coming to see Annie,' replied John, also very angry.

'So am I!'

'Well, you're too late,' said John. 'I've asked her to marry me. And she has said yes.'

'Don't be stupid,' replied Robert. 'She's marrying me!'

'When did you ask her?' asked John.

'On Friday.'

'And did she say yes?'

'Not on Friday. But her answer was to wear white flowers at church this morning.'

'That was for me!' said John.

The quarrel went on for some time.

'Come on,' said John. 'Let's go home. We can't talk in the street. Annie will see us from her window.'

They walked home quickly. And the quarrel went on at

home all afternoon. It got noisier and angrier, and at six o'clock Maggie came into the room. She told the brothers that they must stop fighting at once. She then told them that she was leaving their house for ever.

■ ■ ■ ■ ■

'Why did you do it, my pet?' asked Powell Liversage.

He and Annie Emery were sitting in the garden of his house in Trafalgar Road.

'Why did I do it?' asked Annie. 'Oh, they were so stupid, Powell. I know they're your friends, but really! For ten years they said nothing to me, and then, because of their sister's money, they come to see me. And Powell, they were so stupid. They really thought that I liked them. I wanted them to meet at my house because I wanted to tell them what I thought of them. But I was watching from my bedroom window when they met in the street. They started to quarrel again, and then they went away.'

'They'll be angry with me, I'm afraid,' said Powell. 'When they find out that we're going to get married. They'll say I want to marry you for the . . .'

'I don't want the money, dear,' said Annie. 'They can keep their twelve thousand pounds.'

Powell was a little sorry to hear this, but he said, 'Yes, of course, dearest,' and took Annie's hand.

Just then Powell's mother, who lived with him, came down the garden.

'I don't want the money, dear,' said Annie.
'They can keep their twelve thousand pounds.'

'Powell,' she said. 'John Hessian's here. He wants to see you.'

'I must go,' said Annie. 'I'll go across the fields. Good night, Mrs Liversage. Good night, Powell.'

Liversage went into the house and found John.

'Powell,' he said. 'I've quarrelled with Robert. I can't stay at home. Can I sleep in your spare room?'

'Of course, John, of course.'

'I think I'll go to bed now, if that's all right.'

An hour later there was another knock at the door, and Liversage opened the door to Robert Hessian.

'Hallo, Powell,' said Robert. 'Can I sleep here tonight? I've had a terrible quarrel with John, and Maggie's gone, and I can't stay in the same house as John.'

'But what—'

'Look, I can't talk. I'll go up to your spare room.'

'All right,' said Liversage.

He took Robert up the stairs, opened the door to the spare room, pushed him in, and closed the door.

What a night!

He pushed him in and closed the door.

GLOSSARY

bachelor a man who is not married and has never been married

burglar a person who breaks into houses to steal things

burglary when someone (a burglar) breaks into a house to steal things

castle a big, strong building

coal hard, black stone from under the ground; you burn it on a fire

court a place where the police take criminals (e.g. burglars); the court decides if they must go to prison

elder *(adj)* an elder brother is the older of two brothers

engagement when two people agree to marry

eve the day before (e.g. Christmas Eve is the day before Christmas Day)

fair honest; behaving to people in the right way

frame something made of wood or metal that goes around the outside of a picture

hate to dislike something very strongly; opposite of 'to love'

mad ill in the head

magistrate the most important person in a court, who decides if a person goes free or not

missing not there, or lost

paint *(v)* to make a picture with colours

pet a word you say to someone you like or love very much

portrait a painting of a person

potter a person who makes pottery

pottery plates, cups, etc. made out of clay and then baked

problem something that is very difficult

proof things that show if something is true or not

39

pub a place where people go to drink and meet their friends

quarrel a very angry argument

rid (get rid of) to free yourself of something or someone

servant someone who works in another person's house

service the singing and prayers in a church

slate a flat black stone used for writing on

solicitor a person whose job is helping people with the law

spare *(adj)* a spare room in a house is a room for visitors to
sleep in

stepfather your mother's second husband (not your real father)

success doing something well; in this story, making a lot of
money in business

tail the side of a coin (e.g. a penny) that does not have a picture
of the king's or queen's head on it

toss to throw a coin (e.g. a penny) in the air

widow a woman whose husband has died

will *(n)* a letter to say what a person wants to do with their
money after they are dead

Stories from the Five Towns

ACTIVITIES

Before Reading

1 **Read the back cover of the book. What can you guess about the stories? Tick one box for each sentence.**

	YES	NO
1 The Five Towns are in England.	☐	☐
2 The stories happen in the early 1900s.	☐	☐
3 The people in the stories are all happy.	☐	☐
4 The people in the stories are all poor.	☐	☐
5 The Five Towns are very dangerous.	☐	☐

2 **Read the introduction on the first page of the book. How much do you know now about the stories? Match the people with information.**

Sir Jee / Philip / Toby Hall / John and Robert Hessian

1 . . . are brothers.
2 . . . has a picture of himself.
3 . . . makes a journey by train.
4 . . . is rich.
5 . . . is going to tell his mother something important.
6 . . . don't talk to each other.
7 . . . is going to visit a house in Child Row.
8 . . . have a problem about money.

While Reading

Read *News of the Engagement*. Here are some untrue sentences about the story. Change them into true sentences.

1 Philip asked Agnes to marry him and she said no.
2 In his letters, Philip told his mother he was going to marry Agnes.
3 When Philip opened the door, Agnes was there.
4 Philip didn't like Mr Nixon.
5 When Philip came home from the post office, his mother was alone in the sitting-room.
6 Mr Nixon wanted to marry Agnes.
7 Philip was unhappy about his mother's news.
8 Philip told his mother about Agnes that evening.

Read *The Burglary*. Are these sentences true (T) or false (F)? Rewrite the false ones with the correct information.

1 Sir Jee liked his portrait.
2 The people of the Five Towns gave the portrait to Sir Jee.
3 The police said that William Smith was a burglar.
4 William Smith went to prison for five years.
5 Sir Jee asked William Smith to steal the portrait.
6 Sir Jee opened one of the doors for William Smith.
7 William Smith took the portrait and left the frame.

Read *Beginning the New Year*. Choose the best question-word for these questions, and then answer them.

Why / What / Where / When / Who

1 . . . did Toby Hall miss his train?
2 . . . was Number 11 Child Row a special house for Toby?
3 . . . did Toby marry Priscilla?
4 . . . did the house belong to?
5 . . . did Toby go when he left Priscilla?
6 . . . wrote to Priscilla and told her that Toby was dead?
7 . . . did Toby do when he came back to England?
8 . . . did Priscilla marry when she heard that Toby was dead?
9 . . . was in the picture above the fire?
10 . . . did Toby leave in the house when he went to the pub?.

Read *The Silent Brothers*. Who said these words in the story, and to whom?

1 'We've found your sister's will at last.'
2 'I will say nothing.'
3 'Who shall go first?'
4 'It's very sudden. I must think about it.'
5 'I'm going to church this morning.'
6 'I don't want the money, dear.'

After Reading

News of the Engagement

1 **Philip wrote to Agnes on 23rd December and told her his mother's news. Match these parts of sentences and use the linking words to make a paragraph of five sentences. Then add two sentences, one at the beginning and one at the end of the letter, and the opening and closing words.**

and / because / but / that / when / when

1 _____ posted a letter to you.

2 _____ I wasn't pleased to see him

3 He told me

4 After supper, I went to the post office

5 _____ I arrived home last night,

6 Mr Nixon was still there.

7 _____ I wanted to tell mother about our engagement.

8 my mother looked excited.

9 Our old friend Mr Nixon came to supper,

10 _____ he wanted to marry my mother!

11 _____ I came home again,

The Burglary

2 **A policeman asked Sir Jee some questions about the burglary, but Sir Jee didn't tell the truth about everything. Complete the conversation. Use as many words as you like.**

POLICEMAN: Who was in the house last night?

SIR JEE: I _____.

POLICEMAN: How did the burglar get into the castle?

SIR JEE: Through _____.

POLICEMAN: Did you hear anything in the night?

SIR JEE: No, _____.

POLICEMAN: Did you see anything?

SIR JEE: No, _____.

POLICEMAN: What did the burglar take?

SIR JEE: _____.

POLICEMAN: What happened to the portrait?

SIR JEE: _____.

The policeman thought that Sir Jee's story was very strange. He made some notes about other questions to ask. Use these words to make four more questions. Then write a fifth question of your own.

Why

1 you / alone / castle / Christmas Eve?

2 window open / cold night / December?

3 burglar / make noise / heavy portrait frame?

4 burglar / write / portrait?

Beginning the New Year

3 **Priscilla wrote to her daughter to tell her about Toby Hall. Complete her letter with these words. (Use one word in each gap.)**

America, daughter, dead, die, father, happier, happy, house, left, letter, liked, live, lonely, married, marry, news, potter, tell, unhappy, years

My dear daughter

I have to _____ you some surprising _____. Before I married your father, I _____ a man called Toby Hall. That was twenty-four _____ ago. Toby wasn't _____ because he had to live in my house, so one day he _____ me and went to _____. I wasn't too _____, because I still had my _____ and my money. A year later I got a _____ which said that Toby was _____. So when your father asked me to _____ him, I said yes. We were very happy together, and we had you, our dear _____. But now your _____ is dead and Toby has come back. He didn't _____ in America; he came back to England and worked in Derby as a _____. He wants to _____ here with me again. I think we can be _____ this time. I am _____ without you, and I have always _____ Toby.

With love from

Your mother

4 Here is a new illustration for one of the stories. Find the best place to put the picture, and answer these questions.

The picture goes on page _____, in the story _____.

1 Who are the two men in the picture?
2 Who is the woman looking out of the window?
3 Why are the two men angry?

Now write a caption for the illustration.

Caption: _____

The Silent Brothers

5 **Imagine that Powell Liversage didn't take Robert up to his spare room. Write out their conversation in the correct order and put in the speakers' names. Powell speaks first (number 5).**

1 _____ 'He said that he couldn't stay in the same house as you. What's happened?'

2 _____ 'Why not?'

3 _____ 'Of course I can. She loves me and I love her.'

4 _____ 'Oh no you don't. You just want the twelve thousand pounds.'

5 _____ 'You can't stay here, Robert.'

6 _____ 'You! Powell, you can't marry Annie.'

7 _____ 'Because John's already asleep in the spare room.'

8 _____ 'That's not true. Annie says you and John can have the money. She doesn't want it.'

9 _____ 'Well, I'm afraid she isn't going to marry you, and she isn't going to marry John. She's going to marry me.'

10 _____ 'Why is John in your spare room?'

11 _____ 'Annie said she was going to marry me, but John says she's going to marry him, so we quarrelled.'

6 **Here are some new titles for the stories. Which titles go with which stories? Which titles do you prefer? Why?**

1 *News of the Engagement*   3 *Beginning the New Year*
2 *The Burglary*   4 *The Silent Brothers*

Return from the Dead	An Unlucky Portrait
A Clever Businesswoman	Twelve Thousand Pounds
Two Husbands	The Missed Train
Like Mother, like Son	Mrs Bott's Will
Unhappy Christmas	A Dangerous Plan
A New Father	Happy Christmas

7 **What did you think about the people in these stories? Were they nice or nasty, clever or stupid? Did you feel sorry for anybody? Choose some names, and complete some of these sentences.**

Philip / Philip's mother / Mr Nixon
Sir Jee / William Smith / Lady Dain
Toby Hall / Priscilla
John Hessian / Robert Hessian / Annie Emery /
Powell Liversage / Maggie

1 I feel sorry for _____ because _____.
2 I think _____ was right/wrong to _____.
3 I think _____ did a very bad/nice thing.
4 I think _____ did a very clever/stupid thing.
5 I think _____ was stupider/nicer/nastier than _____.

ABOUT THE AUTHOR

Arnold Bennett was born in 1867 in Hanley, Staffordshire, which was the Hanbridge of his famous 'Five Towns'. His father was a solicitor who wanted his son to be a solicitor too. But when Bennett was 21, he went to London and worked in an office while he was trying to become a writer. He wrote some stories for magazines, and in 1893 he got a job on a famous magazine for women. His first book was *A Man from the North* (1898).

From 1902 to 1912 he lived in Paris, and he married a Frenchwoman, but in the end they did not stay together. His books show that he enjoyed the work of French 'realist' writers (Flaubert and the Goncourt brothers, for example) and that, like them, he wanted to write about the real lives of working people.

Bennett's stories paint a picture of everyday life in the 'Five Towns' of the English Midlands, which became famous in the 1800s for their pottery. He wrote about ordinary people – some of them rich, some of them poor, some clever, some stupid – and his stories are often both funny and sad at the same time. Some of his most famous books are: *Anna of the Five Towns*, *The Old Wives' Tale*, *Clayhanger*, and *The Card*. He also loved the theatre and wrote some very successful plays. He described his own working life in his *Journal*. Arnold Bennett died in 1931.

ABOUT BOOKWORMS

OXFORD BOOKWORMS LIBRARY
Classics • True Stories • Fantasy & Horror • Human Interest
Crime & Mystery • Thriller & Adventure

The OXFORD BOOKWORMS LIBRARY offers a wide range of original and adapted stories, both classic and modern, which take learners from elementary to advanced level through six carefully graded language stages:

Stage 1 (400 headwords)	**Stage 4** (1400 headwords)
Stage 2 (700 headwords)	**Stage 5** (1800 headwords)
Stage 3 (1000 headwords)	**Stage 6** (2500 headwords)

More than fifty titles are also available on cassette, and there are many titles at Stages 1 to 4 which are specially recommended for younger learners. In addition to the introductions and activities in each Bookworm, resource material includes photocopiable test worksheets and Teacher's Handbooks, which contain advice on running a class library and using cassettes, and the answers for the activities in the books.

Several other series are linked to the OXFORD BOOKWORMS LIBRARY. They range from highly illustrated readers for young learners, to playscripts, non-fiction readers, and unsimplified texts for advanced learners.

Oxford Bookworms Starters	*Oxford Bookworms Factfiles*
Oxford Bookworms Playscripts	*Oxford Bookworms Collection*

Details of these series and a full list of all titles in the OXFORD BOOKWORMS LIBRARY can be found in the *Oxford English* catalogues. A selection of titles from the OXFORD BOOKWORMS LIBRARY can be found on the next pages.

New Yorkers

O. HENRY

Retold by Diane Mowat

A housewife, a tramp, a lawyer, a waitress, an actress – ordinary people living ordinary lives in New York at the beginning of this century. The city has changed greatly since that time, but its people are much the same. Some are rich, some are poor, some are happy, some are sad, some have found love, some are looking for love.

O. Henry's famous short stories – sensitive, funny, sympathetic – give us vivid pictures of the everyday lives of these New Yorkers.

The Piano

ROSEMARY BORDER

One day, a farmer tells a farm boy to take everything out of an old building and throw it away. 'It's all rubbish,' he says.

In the middle of all the rubbish, the boy finds a beautiful old piano. He has never played before, but now, when his fingers touch the piano, he begins to play. He closes his eyes and the music comes to him – and the music moves his fingers.

When he opens his eyes again, he knows that his life is changed for ever . . .

BOOKWORMS • CRIME & MYSTERY • STAGE 2

Sherlock Holmes Short Stories

SIR ARTHUR CONAN DOYLE

Retold by Clare West

Sherlock Holmes is the greatest detective of them all. He sits in his room, and smokes his pipe. He listens, and watches, and thinks. He listens to the steps coming up the stairs; he watches the door opening – and he knows what question the stranger will ask.

In these three of his best stories, Holmes has three visitors to the famous flat in Baker Street – visitors who bring their troubles to the only man in the world who can help them.

BOOKWORMS • TRUE STORIES • STAGE 2

The Love of a King

PETER DAINTY

All he wanted to do was to marry the woman he loved. But his country said 'No!'

He was Edward VIII, King of Great Britain, King of India, King of Australia, and King of thirty-nine other countries. And he loved the wrong woman.

She was beautiful and she loved him – but she was already married to another man.

It was a love story that shook the world. The King had to choose: to be King, or to have love . . . and leave his country, never to return.

Henry VIII and his Six Wives

JANET HARDY-GOULD

There were six of them – three Katherines, two Annes, and a Jane. One of them was the King's wife for twenty-four years, another for only a year and a half. One died, two were divorced, and two were beheaded. It was a dangerous, uncertain life.

After the King's death in 1547, his sixth wife finds a box of old letters – one from each of the first five wives. They are sad, angry, frightened letters. They tell the story of what it was like to be the wife of Henry VIII of England.

Tooth and Claw

SAKI

Retold by Rosemary Border

Conradin is ten years old. He lives alone with his aunt. He has two big secrets. The first is that he hates his aunt. The second is that he keeps a small, wild animal in the garden shed. The animal has sharp, white teeth, and it loves fresh blood. Every night, Conradin prays to this animal and asks it to do one thing for him, just one thing.

This collection of short stories is clever, funny, and shows us 'Nature, red in tooth and claw'. In other words, it is Saki at his very best.